My Little Friend®

Goes To The Zoo

By Evelyn M. Finnegan
Illustrations by Margaret Farrell Bruno

LITTLE FRIEND PRESS

SCITUATE, MASSACHUSETTS

First U.S. edition 1997.
Printed in China. Published
in the United States by Little Friend
Press, Scituate, Massachusetts.

ISBN: 1-890453-03-X

Library of Congress
Catalog Card Number: 97-071682

LITTLE FRIEND PRESS
28 NEW DRIFTWAY
SCITUATE, MASSACHUSETTS 02066

To my husband Paul with love.

Today is a great day
to go to the zoo.

We're all together.

I hold Little Friend
in my hand so that he
can see everything we do.

We've come today to see the new baby kangaroo.

We check the map to see where to go and then Dad

leads the way.

Monkey had been watching,
and he thought, is that a banana?

"Wait a minute, you're not a banana!"
"Who is that?" the other monkey asked.

"Are you lost?" "Where do you live?" asked the monkey. Little Friend didn't say anything. Monkey looked puzzled.

"I think he's lost," said monkey. "Don't worry. I'll help you find where you belong."

First they started with the elephants.

"Do you live here, Little Friend?"

The elephant scooped up Little Friend with his trunk and looking into his face said, "Why you're not a peanut!"

"Do you live here Little Friend?"

A huge lion let out a ferocious R..O..A..A..R..!

Monkey quickly raced away with Little Friend
saying, "Whoa, you sure don't want to live here!"

"Excuse me, maybe you can help us, we're looking for Little Friend's home."

The seals tossed Little Friend back and forth, high up in the air until SPLASH!...Little Friend fell into the water.

"Oops, I don't think you're supposed to get wet, let's keep looking."

"Little Friend is this where you live?"

The polar bears stopped and gave them a look saying,
"Absolutely not...you must be joking!"

And they turned and walked into their caves.

Maybe with the giraffes, thought monkey. "Hello, hello up there, can you help us?"

Monkey and Little Friend climbed all the way up to the giraffe's face and asked, "Does Little Friend belong here with you?"

The giraffe shook her head no, sending monkey and Little Friend tumbling down her long neck.

"What about the birds?"
said monkey.

"You're the same color
but where are your wings?"

And so they continued on...

Monkey hoped this might be the right place.

"Penguin does Little Friend belong to you?"
"Certainly not," and all the penguins laughed.

"Can you help us mother kangaroo?"
"Little Friend is lost and we're trying
to find where he lives."

Mother kangaroo picked up Little Friend and
placed him in her pouch. This almost feels
right, thought Little Friend.

Suddenly, the zoo keeper noticed something very unusual in the kangaroo's pouch, "Well, you don't belong in there," and he placed Little Friend in his pocket.

Over the loud speaker came the announcement... "If
anyone finds a yellow Little Friend please return
him to the Lost and Found."

Quickly, monkey reached down and grabbed Little Friend
out of the zoo keeper's pocket.

Who is looking for Little Friend, the monkey wondered.

There waiting at the Lost and Found was the family that monkey had seen earlier sitting on the bench.

"Look, there's Little Friend," they all shouted. Frightened, monkey dropped Little Friend on the ground and quickly scurried up the tree.

Little Friend was happy to be back
where he belonged, safe inside the
secret pocket underneath the sweater.

Monkey was watching...

...he was happy too.

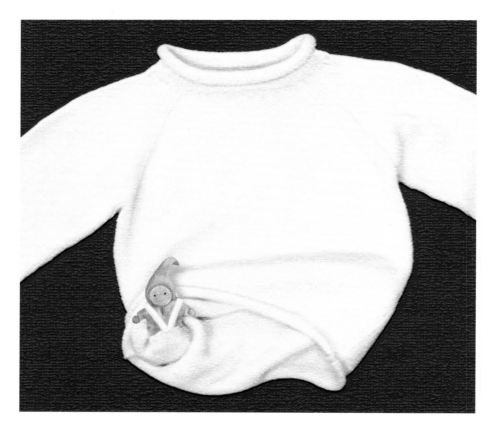

The End.